Welcome to the Party

To my daughter, Kaavia James, and every family whose
journey to baby might've taken a bit longer than expected.
Welcome to the party; you are right on time.—G.U.

To my shining star, Aliciana—A.E.

Welcome to the Party
Text copyright © 2020 by booksbooksbooksGUW, Inc.
Illustrations copyright © 2020 by Ashley Evans
All rights reserved. Printed in the United States of America.
No part of this book may be used or reproduced in any manner whatsoever without written permission except
in the case of brief quotations embodied in critical articles and reviews. For information address HarperCollins
Children's Books, a division of HarperCollins Publishers, 195 Broadway, New York, NY 10007.
www.harpercollinschildrens.com

ISBN 978-0-06-297861-5 (trade bdg) — ISBN 978-0-06-301815-0 (special edition) — ISBN 978-0-06-303730-4 (special edition)

The artist used Procreate and Adobe Photoshop to create the digital illustrations for this book.
Typography by Chelsea C. Donaldson
20 21 22 23 24   PC   10 9 8 7 6 5 4 3 2 1
❖
First Edition

Welcome to the Party

Gabrielle Union
pictures by Ashley Evans

HARPER
An Imprint of HarperCollinsPublishers

SWEET BABY,
there's a party happening,
and it's you who's invited.

From your *Kicks* and your *taps,*

I can tell you're excited.

You're the guest of *honor*.

Let me show you around.

Take my hand
and we'll share
this new LOVE
we have found.

Say hi to your guests.
They're happy to meet you.
They've waited so long
and can't wait to greet you.

STRUT down the red carpet.

The crowd will CHEER loudly.

As you SASHAY and TWIRL,
remember: shine proudly.

Take your place at the table,
topped with everything YUMMY.

Where we'll eat, share *laughs,*

and PLAY kiss the tummy.

The venue is your castle,
and YOU RULE supreme.

There's even a SNUGGLE SPOT
made for you and for me.

Catch a vibe on the dance floor,
feel the sound of the beat.
    We'll always CELEBRATE YOU.
Our world is complete.

After every GUEST leaves,

and all the BALLOONS pop . . .

. . . our ShiNDiG keeps going

and will NEVER, EVER stop.

I love you to iNfiNiTY, with
a smile big and hearty.